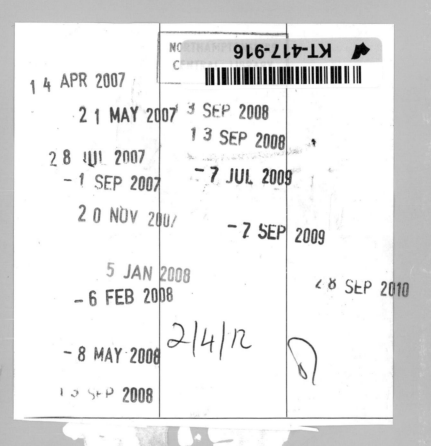

THE AMAZING ADVENTURES OF
HERCULES

Retold by
Claudia Zeff

Adapted by Gill Harvey

Illustrated by
Stephen Cartwright

Reading Consultant: Alison Kelly
University of Surrey Roehampton

Contents

Some pages show you how to say unusual names.
The parts of the words in **bold** should be stressed.

Chapter 1

The jealous goddess

Long ago, the great god Zeus had a baby son called Hercules* with a human. All the other gods loved him, or nearly all...

The goddess Hera* was jealous of Hercules from the start.

3

* say **her**-kew-lees and **hear**-a

"I'll soon get rid of him," thought Hera. She sent some poisonous snakes slithering into his cradle.

Sssssss... arrrggghhh!

But Hercules was already so strong, he strangled the snakes easily. Hera was furious.

As he grew up, Hercules got stronger and stronger. One day, he heard that a wicked lord was stealing cows from the King of Thebes*.

Hercules challenged the lord to a battle. Then he waited on a narrow path and, all on his own, killed the lord's soldiers, one by one.

5

* say **thee**-bz

The King of Thebes was delighted. "Thank you!" he cried. "You may marry my daughter Megera* as a reward."

Mrs. Hercules? Sounds good!

Hercules and Megera were very happy and had three fine sons. Hercules loved teaching them everything he knew.

6

But Hera grew more and more jealous.

I'll put an evil spell on him!

Under her spell, Hercules suddenly went crazy and killed his beloved sons. Then he felt terrible. "What have I done?" he cried.

He rushed to a temple to beg for forgiveness. A priestess listened to his prayer. "You must see King Eurystheus*," she said.

You'll find King Eurystheus in Tiryns*.

"The king will give you twelve tasks," she said. "If you do them all, the gods will forgive you."

8

Chapter 2

The tasks begin

Hercules went to find the king.
"What are my tasks?" he asked.

"There's a huge lion prowling around," said the king.

Your first task is to kill it!

Hercules hunted the lion for a whole month. Finally, he spotted it lurking near a cave. He jumped out and stabbed it with his sword...

... but the lion's skin was too tough. So he hit it over the head with a club.

The lion was stunned, but it was still alive.

Hercules crept after the monstrous beast and followed it into a cave. Suddenly, the lion sprang on top of him.

They rolled around fighting for hours. In the end, Hercules grasped it by the throat, and strangled it.

The king was terrified when he saw the lion.

"Don't worry," said Hercules. "It's dead!"

But the king was so scared, he jumped into a big brass pot. "Go and kill the Hydra*!" he shouted. "That's your next task!"

12

* say **high**-dra

The Hydra was a horrible nine-headed monster that lived in a gloomy marsh. Hercules took his nephew for company. As they set out, the goddess Athene* appeared.

You must shoot flaming arrows to make the Hydra come out.

"One sniff of its poison will kill you, so hold your breath," she said.

* say a-**thee**-nee

Hercules approached the Hydra's lair. He tied bunches of grass to his arrows, and set fire to them. Then he shot them into the cave.

He could hear a scary hissing. The Hydra was coming out! Soon, it was in front of the cave, all nine heads spitting poison.

Hercules held his breath and raced towards the Hydra.

With a mighty blow, he knocked off one of the ugly nine heads. The head screamed loudly and thudded to the ground.

But as it fell, two new heads grew in its place!

Whaaat?

Hercules thought quickly. Then he set fire to his spear and attacked the Hydra again.

As soon as he chopped each head off, he set fire to the neck so that no new heads could grow. At last, the Hydra was dead.

Chapter 3

A stag and a boar

Hercules' third task was to catch a stag with golden antlers. He chased the stag for a year, but it always got away.

Then, one day near a river, he saw something shining in the sun.

"The golden antlers!" he whispered to himself.

Hercules tiptoed down to the river with his net. The stag stood drinking peacefully and didn't see Hercules creeping up on him.

Suddenly, Hercules made a big leap and threw the net over the stag. It was trapped!

The stag fought and struggled until it was tired out. When it lay still at last, Hercules tied its golden hooves together.

"Off we go!" he said, and lifted the stag onto his back.

But as he trudged through the woods, Hercules saw a woman up ahead.

"Stop!" she cried. "I am the goddess Artemis* and that's my stag."

Where are you taking him?

To show King Eurystheus, in Tiryns.

"You may show the king my stag," she said. "But you must promise not to harm it."

"I'll take good care of it," said Hercules, and went on.

* say **are**-te-miss

"Well done, Hercules," said the king. "Now catch a wild boar."

Bring it here alive.

Hercules went to see his friend, the centaur. Half-man, half-horse, he knew where every animal lived.

"Hello Hercules," he cried. "You must head to the mountains. But stay and have a drink first!"

Some time later, Hercules set off. It was a long trek to the mountains and it took hours to track down the boar.

At last, Hercules saw it, perched high on a mountain ledge.

But the boar was enormous and dangerous. However was he going to catch it?

"I'll have to trick it," thought Hercules. Slowly, he drove the boar in front of him... up and up... higher into the mountains.

That's it... I'll soon get you now!

When they reached the snow at the top, the boar was so big and clumsy it fell into a snowdrift.

"Got you!" cried Hercules.

Quickly, he chained up the boar and heaved it onto his back. Then off he staggered to the king.

When the king saw the boar, he jumped back into his pot.

"Your next task is to clean out the stables of King Augeas*... in one day!" he called.

Aaagh! It's huge.

26

Chapter 4

Rivers and birds

King Augeas roared with laughter when he heard the task.

"Come and see my stables," he chuckled. "No one has cleaned them for thirty years!"

One day? Impossible!

King Augeas was right. The
stables were dirty and very smelly.
Hercules had a good look around,
thinking hard. Then he smiled.

"This should be easy,"
he thought.

Early the next day, he started
work. First, he knocked a big hole
at either end of the stables.

Then he climbed a nearby hill.
There, two rivers met and flowed
down a valley. Hercules started
to dam them up with huge rocks.

He worked all day in the hot sun.
By the evening, the rivers ran a
different way, towards the stables.

The rivers gushed through the holes he had made, taking all the dirt with them. In minutes, the stables were sparkling.

Just before sunset, Hercules unblocked the rivers and mended the stable walls. The fifth task was finished.

The sixth task was to kill a flock of terrible birds. The birds ripped animals apart and feasted on them. Sometimes they even ate people. Hercules set off again.

The birds lived on an island in the middle of a marsh. Hercules tried to row there, but the marsh was too muddy. Soon, his boat was stuck.

How could he reach the birds? "Maybe the goddess Athene will help me," he thought. In a flash, she was there.

"Take this golden rattle," she said. "If you shake it, you'll terrify the birds and they will fly up."

When they fly away, you'll be able to shoot them!

The rattle was so loud, Hercules was almost deafened. But it did the trick. Soon the birds were wheeling above him, shrieking in fear.

Back on land, Hercules shot the birds as they flew off their island. He took the biggest to the king.

Chapter 5

Bulls and horses

The bird didn't look very dangerous now it was dead.

"Ha! That's just a little bird," said the king. "Go and catch the great white bull in Crete!"

Crete was an island far away, so Hercules found a ship to sail there. Its ruler, King Minos*, welcomed him and led him into his beautiful palace.

"That bull is a menace," said King Minos. "It's killing people and wrecking the island."

35

Hercules found the bull in an olive grove. It pawed the ground with its monstrous hooves and snorted fire from its nostrils.

As Hercules tried to creep up on it, the bull saw him and charged.

But Hercules was wearing the skin from the lion he had killed and was protected from the bull's fiery breath.

He grabbed the bull's terrible
horns. The bull fought wildly, but
Hercules clung on. At last, the
bull grew tired and collapsed.

When the king saw the bull, he was terrified.

"Bring me the horses of King Diomedes*!" he squeaked to Hercules. "They eat people!"

Hercules? I'm Diomedes. Come on in, my friend...

So, Hercules went to Diomedes' castle, taking four friends with him. Diomedes seemed friendly, but Hercules didn't trust him.

* say die-oh-**mee**-deez

"I think Diomedes plans to kill us," he told his friends. "We'll have to get the horses tonight."

When it was dark, they crept down to the stables.

Hercules broke down the stable doors. The savage horses were chained to a beam and he quickly chopped them free.

Hercules and his friends hurried to their ship with the horses. But before they could escape, King Diomedes heard what they'd done.

He grabbed some soldiers and rushed after Hercules.

Diomedes was no match for
Hercules and his friends.
Soon, all the soldiers
were dead. Hercules
himself killed
Diomedes and
gave him to
the horses.

Once the horses had gobbled
Diomedes up, they became quite
tame. "Now, back to that silly
king in his pot!" said Hercules.

Chapter 6

Amazons and ogres

Hercules' ninth task was to fetch the belt of Hippolyta*, Queen of the Amazons. The Amazons were fierce women warriors and no one had ever seen them.

Hercules took a ship full of brave men to hunt for them.

42

* say hip-**pol**-it-ta

To Hercules' surprise, Hippolyta was friendly. "I've come for your belt," he told her.

"You won't need to fight for it," she said, with a smile.

She laid out a wonderful feast for Hercules and his crew.

But the goddess Hera was still jealous of Hercules. She hated to see him having fun.

So, she disguised herself as an Amazon and joined the feast. "Hercules is here to kill our Queen," she whispered to the women.

Don't trust him!

The Amazons jumped to their feet. They attacked Hercules and his men with their swords.

In the fight, Hercules killed Hippolyta. He grabbed her belt and ran. "Back to the ship!" he roared to his men.

But the Amazons charged after them. A terrible battle began.

For hours, it looked as though the Amazons would win. Hercules and his men fought on.

In the end, the fierce women were defeated, but many men were badly hurt. Feeling very tired, they headed for home.

The men could rest, but
Hercules still had three
tasks to go.

"Find Geryon*,
the three-headed
ogre, and bring
me his cows,"
said the king.

Geryon lived on an island near
Africa. It meant another long
and tiring journey.

Helios*, the sun god, felt sorry

for Hercules.
He sent him
a water lily
chariot to
use as a
boat.

48

* say **gair**-ree-on and **hee**-lee-us

Hercules explored Geryon's island and soon spotted the ogre and his cows. But before he could  get to them, a ferocious two-headed dog jumped out at him.

Hercules whacked the dog with his club. The heavy blow killed it at once.

Hercules went on towards the cows. The ogre was standing in the middle of their field.

Hercules hid behind a rock and fitted a poisoned arrow to his bow.

As he stood, the ogre would be difficult to hit.

"Geryon!" Hercules yelled and the ogre turned. Quickly, Hercules fired his arrow, sending it right through all three bodies.

Geryon dropped down, dead. Hercules herded the cows onto the water lily boat and hurried back to the king.

Chapter 7

Two tasks to go

"You took too long," said the king, grumpily. "Go and find the Tree of the Hesperides*. I want three of its golden apples."

The tree was at the end of the Earth, where a great giant, Atlas, held up the sky.

* say hess-**pair**-i-deez

"How can I get the apples?" Hercules asked him.

"First, you must kill the dragon guarding the tree," said Atlas. "But I'm the only one who can pick the apples."

Hercules found the dragon, shot it dead and went back to Atlas.

"Now, if you would hold up the sky for me, I'll go and pick the apples," said the giant.

Hercules waited... and waited...

Atlas took his time picking the apples. He was in no hurry to go back to holding up the sky.

I'll offer to take the apples to the king myself!

But Hercules was too clever for Atlas. "Before you go to the king, can you show me again how I should hold the sky?" he asked.

The eleven tasks had taken ten years. Hercules was exhausted and there was still one task to go.

"Fetch Cerberus*," said the king.

"But that's the dog that guards the Underworld!" Hercules gasped.

Don't worry. We'll help.

It seemed impossible, but the gods Hermes* and Athene offered to show him the way.

* say **sir**-bir-uss and **her**-meez

After a long, gloomy journey, they reached the river Styx*. They had to cross it to reach the Underworld, but Charon*, the old ferryman, wouldn't take them.

In the end, Charon agreed to take Hercules, but he wouldn't let Hermes or Athene on board.

* say sticks and **kair**-on

Hercules landed safely on the other side and wandered among the ghosts. They whispered in strange, faded voices.

He walked on through the land of the dead until he reached the King and Queen. He knelt down before them and asked for the dog.

"I'll take care of him," promised Hercules and hurried back to the river Styx to find Cerberus.

Cerberus stood at the gate to the Underworld. Each of his three heads had a mane of writhing, hissing snakes. He was truly terrifying.

As Hercules stepped closer, Cerberus leaped. Hercules flung himself forward and grabbed the dog.

After a long struggle, the dog sank to the ground, defeated.

Hercules took him across the river Styx and all the way back to King Eurystheus.

Here is Cerberus. I have finished my twelve tasks!

As always, the king wasn't that pleased to see him.

Hercules went straight to the temple to see the priestess.

"The gods have forgiven you for killing your sons," she said.

The other gods were proud of Hercules. They welcomed him to their home on Mount Olympus and kept him safe on all of his adventures from then on.

Try these other books in
Series Two:

Jason and the Argonauts: Jason's uncle
has sent him to fetch the golden fleece of a
flying ram. Jason knew it would be tricky.
But even he didn't expect to face man-
eating birds and a murdering king.

The Amazing Adventures of Ulysses:
Ulysses sets out to rescue a Greek princess
and ends up in a ten-year war. But when he
tries to get home, his problems really start.

King Arthur: Arthur is just a boy, until
he pulls a sword out of a stone. Suddenly,
he is King of England. The trouble is,
not everyone wants him on the throne.

The Fairground Ghost: When Jake goes
to the fair he wants a really scary ride.
But first, he must teach the fairground
ghost a trick or two.

The story of Hercules was first told about 3,000 years ago in Ancient Greece. Hercules was the Greeks' strongest hero, though they called him Heracles. Hercules is his Roman name and we have used it because he is much better known by this name today.

Series editor: Lesley Sims
Designed by
Katarina Dragoslavić

This edition first published in 2007 by Usborne Publishing Ltd.,
Usborne House, 83-85 Saffron Hill, London EC1N 8RT, England.
www.usborne.com
Copyright © 2007, 2003, 1982, Usborne Publishing Ltd.